QATAR CAPER

YEAR 3021

UMM AISHA

UMM AISHA

CONTENTS

DOHA QATAR A HUNDRED YEARS FROM TODAY

In 3021, Qatar is the richest country in the world.

There are Islamic holistic healing centres on camel farms. The country follows the Sharia law and Islamic custom and tradition.

It is the 31st century, and many changes have taken place in the desert city. Qatar of the future is blessed with seasonal rain, and taking advantage of the short monsoon season, several Qataris with their foresight have harvested the rainwater and nurtured crops and vegetable farms

One of the most iconic spots in Qatar is the mangroves of Al-Thakhira where you could float on water standing with the Glide-Water shoes. It was a great way to explore the waterbody on the surface.

In 3020, technology has taken the lead in Doha, and the city's construction has taken a futuristic shape. 'The Pearl' is the tallest building in the world; it is 998 meters tall and comprises 201 floors.

In the year 2070, the Quran garden was inaugurated by the ruling Sheikh. In the Quran garden, virtual reality technology is used to enact each story while a robot narrates the events from 'The Book of Prophets' written by Al-Imam Ibn Kathir. Colourful murals are on the walls in the area that encloses each Quran story in its space. The picnic area has stone grills with community marble tables and seats.

Besides the Quran garden, the government has built an underground aquarium in Corniche and a massive futuristic zoo near Al-Kharab. Each attraction functions with the latest technology and robotic teams to assist the visitors.

CHAPTER 1 -METALLICA AND THE FOUR CHILDREN

Hamza and Fariha looked outside the window of the flying Aero-car, the futuristic car was a gift to Zuni from her father. They could see the pod taxis suspended in the air moving at lightning speed to their destinations.

Both Hamza and Fariha had dark, curly hair and brown eyes. Hamza was reserved, while Fariha was lively and animated in her interactions.

Hamza's parents, Farida and Hamad bin Khoury, migrated to Doha when Hamza's elder brother, Ameer, was just ten years old. Hamad was once a wealthy businessman who owned several properties in his home country. But when there was unrest in his country, he had to leave his home and migrate to Doha.

In the past, Zuni's father, Nawaf Sheikh, was Hamad's close friend and business partner. But Hamad Bin Khoury had to leave his business behind because of the war in his country. He now worked in the Qatari government office. Hamza's twin sister, Fariha, was Zuni's best friend

Khaled checked the time on his digital wristwatch with his detail-attentive eyes. He was strong and sturdy for his age but gentle like a kitten.

Khaled was a good-humoured kid and it was also amazing how he often pointed out the bright side of any situation. Khaled Mohammed came from an affluent family, and his villa was next door to Zuni's.

Zuni had a fun-loving personality, straight black hair, and bright black eyes that twinkled each time she smiled. Every day, Zuni's personal robot Metallica drove the young girl to school in the hover-car.

Zuni spoke excitedly to her friends as Metallica turned the hover-car sharply around the tenth floor of the three hundred feet Aspire Tower.

Zuni too came from a wealthy family. Her parents, Zaira and Nawaf Sheikh often travelled around the world with their five kids: Zuni and her four elder brothers.

Metallica glanced upwards, and in a microsecond, counted the floors of the tall building. She spoke in her metallic voice, "Do you know the Aspire tower has thirty-six floors?"

The children politely turned their heads to listen to Metallica as she rattled off the information about the building.

Fariha looked outside her window and pointed at the sea; they were over the Corniche. The sea on their right side looked blue and dazzling in the bright sunlight.

The hover-car started descending as they caught sight of the tall QIS building with its glinting glass windows on the horizon.

Metallica stopped at the drop point and waited patiently for the children to alight. As soon as the children stepped out of the car, the doors automatically locked.

The four friends then made a mad dash towards their classroom.

CHAPTER 2-TEST RESULTS

Fariha, Hamza, Khaled, and Zuni were classmates in grade three. The four friends attended the Qatar International School. QIS stretched across a huge campus with the latest international curriculum.

The Doha Government had made education and health care free for all. Most of the children living in Qatar attended QIS, irrespective of their parents' financial status.

On getting to the classroom, they sat hurriedly and thanked God they had got to class just in time.

The moment their class teacher, Miss Rabia, who also taught robotic science, entered the classroom, all twenty students got up to wish her a good morning.

It was time for the roll calls, and each student responded to their names as Miss Rabia called out loudly.

At that moment, their school robot entered the room, whirring on its wheels, and deposited a stack of foldable Net-Books on Miss Rabia's desk.

Miss Rabia politely thanked the robot and distributed the corrected test marks to her class.

As expected, Fariha and Khaled had topped the class. Zuni and Hamza had also done well in the test, but their class bully, Zimran, was at the bottom of the list.

Zuni whispered to her friends, "Guys, there's a treat at my place today after school."

After school, as soon as the Aero-car stopped outside her door Zuni ran inside her home. Metallica beeped in alarm at Zuni's haste.

Zuni said 'Salaam alaikum' when she saw her elegant mother and hugged her while handing the test results to her mom. Zaira hugged her daughter back.

Zuni said, "Ammi, I have called my three friends; Fariha, Hamza, and Khaled for tea today. Will you please ask the cook to make something sweet as a treat for them?"
Her mother smiled indulgently and said she would talk to the cook.

Later in the evening, Fariha, Hamza, and Khaled got to Zuni's home. They greeted Zaira and shared their test marks with her.

Zaira treated them to a wonderful feast of Qatar's traditional sweet dishes like Kunafa and Esh Asaraya.
The children happily scraped off their bowls and declared they wouldn't mind exams if they could have treats for each test's result at Zuni's home

CHAPTER 3-THE MISSING MEHALABIYA

On Qatar National day, Fariha, Hamza, Khaled, and Zuni entered Qatar Grand Mosque's Community centre, bright and early.

Their parents were talking to the other elders while the children waited eagerly for the caretaker at the centre to serve them the sweet and creamy Mehalabiya.

Just then, the hired cook entered the main sanitarium, and there was a heated discussion with the young student Imam.

Someone had eaten from a few of the Mehalabiya bowls. The cook had lined up the bowls on an enormous round tray and stepped out of the kitchen.

When he returned, he noticed some of the bowls were empty.

On hearing this, the Imam went with the cook to confirm the situation, and they were shocked to see four more empty bowls.

The young Imam - caretaker said thoughtfully while stroking his beard, "This is serious."

Hamza, Zuni, and Khaled had followed the two grown-ups and saw the empty bowls with the disappeared Mehalabiya.

The mystery of the missing Mehalabiya baffled the children, and they decided to search for clues to catch the culprit.

While the cook and the Masjid caretaker spoke to each other, Fariha, Hamza, Zuni and Khaled looked around cautiously for any clue they could find.

With her sharp eyes, Fariha saw drops of a thick creamy substance leading down the spiral staircase that led the centre's backside area.

She nudged her friend, Zuni, and the two boys came to see what Fariha had found.

When they saw drops of Mehalabiya, they followed the trail down the spiral staircase until they reached the courtyard.

The green lawn in the courtyard sparkled under the sun's bright rays, and the waist-high bushes looked cool and inviting.

Khaled noticed a movement in the bush near the date palm tree, and he silently signalled the others to follow him. They tip-toed towards the palm trees, and Hamza quietly pushed back a shrub. The boys roared angrily while the girls screamed in fright.

CHAPTER 4 – THE CHILDREN SOLVE A MYSTERY

The commotion terrified Zimran and his brother, Jamaal, and they dropped their bowls full of Mehalabiya on the green lawn.

Hamza and Khaled scowled at Zimran and demanded the two brothers admit to the Masjid cook that they had pilfered the bowls filled with the sweet dish.

Zimran's brother, Jamaal, was terrified at being caught, so he burst into tears.

On hearing the commotion, the caretaker came rushing to the courtyard. When he saw Jamaal crying with an empty bowl of Mehalabiya in his hand, he understood the situation and told the children to come inside the Masjid premises.

The six children followed the young Imam - caretaker inside the mosque.
Jamaal was seven years old; he was just a year younger than Zimran. He sobbed uncontrollably and said he was sorry. Zimran also apologised.

When Zimran's mother, Sarah, entered the Grand Mosque centre, she saw her sons sitting quietly on the floor mats. Sarah spoke sternly and asked Zimran why he ate the Mehalabiya without permission.

"We both were hungry, and there was nothing nice to eat,"

Zimran said tearfully.

Bewildered, Sarah regarded her sons and said, "But our cook, Rutba, had cooked Mehalabiya for breakfast.

They chorused, "Her food isn't tasty." Zimran then added, "I noticed Rutba adding salt instead of sugar in the Mehalabiya pot, and when I pointed out her mistake, she quickly dumped the entire tin of sugar in the vessel."

Zimran's parents were scientists with the Qatari government, and each one had a busy schedule. Sarah and her husband usually ate from their office cafeteria because of their tight schedule.

Sarah looked at Zimran as a new understanding dawned on her. All those uneaten meals. She promised to look into the matter, and Zimran and Jamaal felt better after hearing this.

Fariha, Hamza, Khaled, and Zuni, who were all watching the course of events between Zimran and his mother, congratulated one another. They then heaved a sigh.

"At least, grade three lunch boxes will now be safe," Zuni said.

CHAPTER 5- FARIHA ADOPTS A KITTEN

Fariha was enjoying walking down West-bay Street after visiting Zuni at her house.

It was a school holiday on Saturday, and both girls had spent their afternoon playing with Zuni's dollhouse.

White clouds scudded over the azure Qatari sky and a bright sun shone down on the streets of the desert city.

Khaled and Hamza had gone to Al-Rayyan with Khaled's father to attend a friend's "Qur'an completion party." The parents organised the party in honour of their child completing the Qur'an recitation for the first time.

Khaled and Hamza had already completed the Qur'an the year before, so their parents organised the party for each of them within the gap of one month.

Fariha was all alone on the street when she heard a strange mewling behind a bush. She immediately strained her ears at the sound. After listening to the strange sound for a few seconds, she bent down and saw a scared tiny white kitten hiding behind the bush.

Fariha kneeled down on the cobbled footpath and started calling out to the kitten. The kitten immediately ran to the little girl and leapt on her lap.

" Awwww, kitty," said Fariha.

"Meeeeeeoooowwww," replied the kitten, rubbing its head on Fariha's knee.

Fariha rubbed her cheek on the kitten's back, "Your voice is so sweet and with your white fur you remind me of my Meesha doll. That's it, I will call you Meesha. I hope you like your name kitty?"

The kitten purred happily in reply to Fariha's query.

The little girl felt happy the kitten had liked the name she gave her and holding the kitten in the crook of her arm Fariha marched two streets down to her home.

When Fariha got home, her mother felt worried the kitten might be someone's pet. But after Khaled and Hamza had asked at a few houses on the street where Fariha had found Meesha, it was satisfactorily declared that it was a lost kitten.

The boys then told Fariha she could safely adopt Meesha. Hamad, Fariha's father, arranged with the vet to have the kitten vaccinated and later took the children to buy cat food at the pet store.

The kitten, Meesha, never left Fariha's side, and always followed her everywhere on her small kitten feet.

CHAPTER 6- ZUNI AND HER ROBOTIC SCIENCE HOMEWORK

Miss Rabia was the class teacher for grade three, and she was well-known for her strictness. The children behaved obediently during her lessons and avoided talking to each other as Miss Rabia frowned at any kind of disturbance in her class.

Zuni was one of Miss Rabia's favourite students, but she was still cautious not to irk her science teacher and feared her as much as other students did.

However, Iqbal was also Miss Rabia's favourite student. He was an Indian expatriate whose mother worked in the administrative department in QIS, and Iqbal's mother was a close friend of Miss Rabia.

Over the weekend, Miss Rabia had given her students an assignment. Each student was supplied with a mechanised kit, and they had to assemble the kits to create tiny robots using the instruction manual.

The children would be graded on how well the automaton functioned and followed their instructions, and the assignment had to be submitted on Monday, during the Robotic Science class.

Post-lunch, Miss Rabia entered the classroom, and the students stood up to wish her a good afternoon. Miss Rabia then instructed them to keep their assembled robots on their desks.

The students rummaged in their desks for their science books along with the robot project. Shortly, each student had their completed robots on their desks, and each machine had the dimension of a tennis ball. Unfortunately, Zuni could not find the robot she had put together over the weekend.

She urgently whispered to Fariha, who whispered back, "Are you sure you had kept the machine in your desk?"

Zuni nodded and looked around desperately. She then clutched Fariha's arm in astonishment and pointed to the boy who sat across them - it was Iqbal, Miss Rabia's favourite student. He had her robot on his desk.

For Zuni's automaton to be different from others, she had tied a pink ribbon on its hand. She watched in horror as her machine sat on Iqbal's desk, and he was already getting it signed by Miss Rabia.

 Zuni got up from her seat and said vociferously, "That is my robot."
Miss Rabia looked puzzled and asked her, " What do you mean it is yours? It is Iqbal's robot."

 Zuni persisted, saying she had tied the tiny pink ribbon around the robot's hand.

Iqbal reddened but quickly recovered and said slyly, " Teacher, maybe Zuni forgot her homework."

Zuni was furious at the implication. She burst out angrily, " Iqbal, you fibber, that is my robot, and I want it back!"

Miss Rabia frowned and said crossly, "Enough, Zuni. If you don't have your machine ready by the time I reach your desk, I will send a note to your parents."

Miss Rabia's angry tone stunned Zuni into silence, but she tried to speak once again.

"Enough, Zuni," Miss Rabia spoke irritably.

The young girl sat down quietly, blinking back furious tears. As she did not have her robot ready when Miss Rabia reached her desk, Zuni got a remark in her school diary for her parents to sign.

After a while, the school principal, Mr Roberts, entered Zuni's class to check out the children's project. Each child brought their robot to the teacher's desk and presented its function; the kit had a remote control wired to the robot's sensors.

When it was Iqbal's turn, he proudly picked up the robot and went to the front of the classroom.

Fariha, Khalid, and Hamza stood next to Zuni, clearly annoyed for their friend.

Iqbal kept the robot on their teacher's table and clicked the remote. Zilch! There was no response. The robot did not move. Mr Roberts waited patiently for the boy to correct his mistake.

Miss Rabia looked perplexed because it was a simple project, and the parts of the kit came with an instruction manual which the children had practised in her previous class.

Zuni triumphantly looked at Iqbal's bewildered face and marched up to Miss Rabia's desk.

She spoke confidently, "This robot will not function with the remote because it is voice-automated.

CHAPTER 7-IQBAL'S CONFESSION

Iqbal's face paled, and he looked terrified.

It was time for Mr Roberts to look bewildered as the young girl voiced her command, and the robot came alive and followed her instructions.

Iqbal wished he could disappear as Miss Rabia incredulously looked at him, furious at his blatant lie.

Miss Rabia turned to Zuni and apologised, "I am sorry Zuni. I should have looked into the matter."

Mr Roberts was briefed, and Iqbal had to confess.

He said he had tried to follow the manual, but the instructions were difficult to understand. He entered the classroom in the morning and his robot had malfunctioned when he made one last attempt to set it up.

But then, he saw Zuni's completed robot sitting on her desk. He was all alone that moment as the children had left the classroom for the first-morning break.

Iqbal quickly took the machine from Zuni's desk so he wouldn't fail in Robotic Science and disappoint his parents.

Mr Roberts asked Iqbal to see him in the office later during the short break. Zuni got an A+ for her work, and she was thrilled with her grade.

Miss Rabia told Zuni to get her diary, and she cancelled the note she wrote in it. She then spoke severely and asked Iqbal to get his diary. In the diary, she put down a note requesting a meeting with Iqbal's parents.

After Miss Rabia left the class, things quietened down, and the students got busy with their next class. Except for poor Iqbal, who was sniffling in his seat, fearful of what his parents would say when they see the note.

Later, Mr Roberts spoke to Iqbal and pointed out that low marks on a project were something his parents would understand, but cheating and stealing were serious crimes. And his parents would be truly disappointed if they knew their son had committed these sins and offences.

Iqbal was ashamed of his behaviour, so he later sought out Zuni and apologised to her, Zuni was a good-natured girl and she forgave him immediately.

Zuni also added that she could aid Iqbal with his projects if he wanted her help. Iqbal thanked her and said Miss Rabia had planned to give him extra classes twice a week after school till he caught up with the others.

After school, Zuni and her friends Fariha, Hamza, and Khaled took their robots back to Zuni's home and raced them till their power ran down.

HI!

CHAPTER 8- MEZZE PARTY

There was a lively atmosphere at Zuni's home. Her mother, Zaira, had invited Zuni's friends for a Mezze party.

Their chef, Gulnaz, was a fantastic cook and the children loved to attend Zuni's get-togethers. After speaking to her friends, Zuni decided to hold the party on a Friday evening.

Khaled, Hamza, and Fariha reached Zuni's home on time. Meesha had also accompanied the children as Zuni had invited the kitten too. Metallica opened the door, and Zuni's mother welcomed the children warmly.

Fariha wore a white dress and she had tied a white ribbon on Meesha's neck to match her dress.

Khaled, Fariha and Hamza greeted Zaira, and Zuni's mother replied cheerfully to all three children with a Walekum-As-Salaam, however the moment she saw Fariha and Meesha wearing the same colour she rained compliments on how pretty and adorable the young girl looked with Meesha in her hands.

"Thank you. ah... hmmm... and Meesha says thank you too," Fariha responded shyly and faltering slightly to her friend's mother's fervent praises.

The boys grinned when they saw Fariha turning red with embarrassment, all three children entered the house and saw Zuni waiting excitedly for them.

For some time, the children played indoor games.

Zuni got her Quran Challenge game out, and they played till Khaled won all three rounds. No one could beat the enthusiasm of this boy in the Quran Challenge game. Khaled said when he grew up, he would one day be a scientist and a Qur'an Hafiz. No one who knew Khaled could argue with him because they knew he was intelligent and also enthusiastic about acquiring in-depth knowledge about Islam.

Just when they were contemplating playing another board game, Zaira entered Zuni's playroom and announced the Mezze was ready. After keeping all the games back in their place, the four children and the kitten, Meesha, scampered down the stairs, towards the dining room.

Fariha and Zuni sat down first, and then Khaled and Hamza took their seats at the dining table. Metallica entered with platters of delicious food comprising dips, pink Zahav, creamy Hummus, Red Muhammara, and white Téhini sauce after everyone was seated. Each dip had pools of green olive oil with pomegranate seeds, and Zaatar sprinkled on top.

A few minutes later, Metallica brought in Falafels, grilled chicken, Shish Touk Kebabs, and tabbouleh salad. On the dining table was an assortment of loaves of bread like Lavash, Pita bread, and even garlic bread, and some had onion seeds sprinkled on top.

The children tasted every dish on the table.

Meesha got a separate bowl of cat food, and she also purred in delight, declaring in her tiny voice that it was the best meal she had ever tasted.

CHAPTER 9- THE MERCY RESTAURANT

Like every Muslim who wished to earn Allah's pleasure, Khaled's father, Aqeb, also did many charities.

Once, while he and Khaled were on their way to visit a relative, their car driver, Abdul, told them about a family-run Indian restaurant in Ad-Dawhah area. The restaurant was named after their ancestral surname, Ansari Brothers - Mercy Restaurant.

The three brothers had migrated from Kerala to Qatar nearly thirty years back. Now, their children helped run the restaurant. The unique thing about Mercy restaurant was that poor labourers working at a minimum wage could eat in the diner for free if they did not have enough money to pay their food bill.

Intrigued, Aqeb decided to explore this place. Later that week, Khaled's father dressed in a modest thobe and visited Mercy restaurant. He walked through the single wooden door entrance of the restaurant.

When he sat down at a table, he looked around; it was a humble and practical place with no frills. The restaurant had plastic tables and chairs. Even though it was bustling with many people who had come to eat their mid-day meal there, the place was clean, and the people serving the food were polite.

Aqeb understood that the people who ran the restaurant were not too well off and might need aid. He then placed an order for the rice plate as it was popular amongst the labourers.

A steel plate was placed in front of him. On one side was a heap of rice, vegetables, and a bowl containing yellow lentils.

After he had eaten his food, he waited for the bill. To his surprise, the waiter politely pointed towards a box kept near the door.

Aqeb was informed that the restaurant owners did not bill their customers, but the patrons could add whatever money they could afford in the money box.

The Ansari family's generosity and trust in the natural goodness of people impressed Aqeb. He requested to see the owner.

At Aqeb's request, the attendant looked worried. He thought Aqeb was upset about something.

Wahab Ansari came out of the kitchen, wiping his hands on a napkin. His head was covered with a cap, and white hair strands peeked out from under the cotton skullcap. He was the oldest of the three brothers.

Aqeb shook hands with him. Meanwhile, Wahab's brothers came out, puzzled at Aqeb's request. He introduced himself to the three brothers and reached for an envelope in his thobe pocket. He then placed it in Wahab's hand and said, "This is to help run your restaurant; a small token for all the good work your family is doing."

After saying this, Aqeb gently walked out of the restaurant. As he walked to his car, he thought of adding the restaurant to his list of charities.

Wahab Ansari and his brothers opened the envelope and found ten thousand riyals inside the packet.

The three brothers hugged each other and thanked Allah

for his help.

"Didn't I tell you all to keep your trust in Allah? For the Most Merciful's help is always near. Now, we no longer have to think about closing down this restaurant," Wahab said to his brothers, who stood in awe of all that had happened.

At Khaled's father's gesture, the brothers felt amazed and at the same time, they felt humbled too.

The brothers went back to serving food to the poor, with a prayer of thanks on their lips.

CHAPTER 9-VISIT TO THE SOUK WAQIF

Farida crinkled her nose as she checked the paper in her hand for the second time; she wanted to ensure her list covered everything.

It was a Saturday, her family was at home, and it was the perfect day to visit the market and purchase spices, dry fruits, and nuts from the merchants in the Souk Waqif - the oldest market in Doha.

Hamza's parents, Hamad and Farida, and the twins were in the car as they drove to the old market. Hamza's older brother, Ameer, could not go with them as he had planned to meet his friends.

Farida loved the old-world charm of the bazaar. Fariha also enjoyed the visit as there was so much to see.

The woody, zesty fragrance of the hundreds of spices competed with sweet heady Arabian perfumes that hung in the air. Glass lanterns dangled outside the shops and the glasses twinkled in red, blue, green, and gold colours.

The streets seemed like mazes to Fariha, and the never-ending shops were filled with clothes, jewellery, perfumes, and Arabian delicacies.

They parked the car some metres away and walked down the labyrinth streets.

Farida made a beeline to the dry fruit stores and bought

dried apricots, sour lemon slices, and sweet round figs tied in a cluster. She also added dates, almonds, walnuts, and pine nuts to her purchase.

She then picked up packets of spices and their ready mixtures like cloves, cinnamon, sumac, Baharat, and Harissa blends.

Farida ended her purchase with a bottle of Zaffran and fresh Zaatar.

Hamad decided it would be better to keep the bags in the car while Hamza, Fariha, and Farida stayed back in the Souk.

Farida took the kids to a coffee shop and waited for Hamad to join them. The fragrant Arabic coffee was served to them from a copper pot and poured into small cups. A plate of Turkish delights was also served along with the coffee.

Fariha daintily nibbled on a red-coloured Turkish delight while Farida sipped on her coffee Ariha.
Hamad soon joined them, and after a cup of coffee each and sweet, sugar-coated Turkish Delights, they explored the market further.

Farida wanted to buy headscarves and Arabic perfumes for herself and Fariha, while Hamad planned to visit the Thobe store with Hamza.

After deciding on a meeting point, the four dispersed in different directions.

Farida was firm on finishing her shopping as next month was Ramadan, and she knew it would be a hectic time for her.

After a few hours, the family finished their shopping and met for a late lunch at Al-Royhan restaurant. They chatted while waiting for their food to be served.

Within a few minutes, the waiter appeared with a tray from the kitchen and placed their order of Chicken Kabsa rice and Chicken Dajjaj with fresh pita bread and a tabbouleh salad on their table.

After their meal was over, Hamad ordered ice cream sundaes for everyone.

Fariha and Hamza cheered for their father as goblets of delicious-looking ice-cream scoops graced their table. The ice cream was swiftly finished, and the family left the restaurant, pleased with their meal.

Later in the evening, they observed the Asr Salah in Souk Waqif mosque, where they had previously observed Zawhar Salah.

On the way back from the mosque, Farida and Fariha told Hamad and Hamza about their purchases. Fariha was especially pleased with the pink scarf her mother had bought for her because of the tiny pearls stitched over it.

The family returned home, tired but pleased with their visit to Souk Waqif.

CHAPTER 11- RAMADAN

Ramadan was the month of mercy that descended on Doha just as winter spread its cool wings on the desert city. Daytimes were pleasantly cool while the nights were chilly.

A peculiar flurry of activities overtook households in Qatar. An urgency was felt in every home in the desert city, and the ladies fussed about all things, big and small.

Even though each family had prepared in advance to welcome the beloved month, there was still so much to do. Zaira instructed her house cook, Gulnaz, to prepare delicacies and refrigerate them for the Ramadan month.

Metallica was excellent at packing the food; however, no one expected the robot to prepare a meal, for her cooking skills were doubtful at the least.

Farida packed her meals in various sized containers and refrigerated them. In preparation for the holy month, Araba hired extra help to clean the house and help in the kitchen.
When the moon was declared, a serene quiet fell over the city like a warm furry sheet. Men, women, and children went to the mosque closest to them for the special night prayers unique to Ramadan.

The days were short and the nights long, and before long half the month got over.

CHAPTER 12-SUHOOR WITH HAMZA

On the fifteenth day of Ramadan, when Hamza's mother woke him for Sehri, he looked out into the dark desert sky. The stars shone brightly, suspended in the universe; they looked like a million fairy lights that twinkled far-far-away.

Just two weeks back, when Ramadan had been declared after the new moon was sighted, Hamza had left with his family to observe Tarawih at their local mosque.

Hamza sat by the window and remembered the story of Prophet Ibrahim (Alaihi Salaam). He then looked at the dark sky and contemplated what was beyond the planets and stars and their One Creator - Allah.

Suddenly, his mother's voice pierced through his ears. It was time for Sehri. He left his window seat and entered the dining room.

The Sehri meal was set. There were dates, fresh fruits, Tehmiha, and cheese with bread. Hamza ate a few pieces of the sweet melon his mother had cut for their meal and a bowl of Tehmiha. He knew the Suhoor or the pre-dawn meal was an essential ritual of Saum-fasting.

It was still dark when he had finished his meal, and Fariha was still eating from her Tehmiha bowl.

Hamza excused himself and went back to his room. There was still time for Adhaan, and the night sky looked brilliant.

Hamza removed his diary and wrote:

The night sky resembles a dark velvety drape that extends as far as my eyes can see.

The stars that shine like sequins are millions, and surely, I cannot count these.

The planets that appear like diamonds look like lamps lost at the sea.

Oh! Our Mighty Lord, how beautifully You have created. For surely there is none comparable to Thee."

At that moment, the Adhaan sounded. Hamza swiftly scribbled the date at the bottom of his most recent poem's page and went into the bathroom to do his Wudu.

For the evening meal, Farida had prepared mutton Kofta with Tzatziki, Thareed, and Machboos. Fariha loved eating Luqaimat, so her mother had made lots of the sweet spongy balls dipped in a saffron and sugar syrup.

The family sat together at the food-laden table, and all five members prayed for the war to end in their home country and peace to prevail. Hamza's father, Hamad, prayed for his extended family to be safe from harm and hoped to be united with them soon.

Once they heard the evening Adhaan, Hamad passed dates to his family. Immediately they said the dua for breaking the fast, they all ate their sumptuous meal before the family prayed their Maghreb Salah.

CHAPTER 13-EID-UL-FITR

Ramadan flew with speed. The Eid moon was sighted, and people prepared for the next day's celebrations.

Schools and offices were closed, and the city took on a festive look.

Each house had the fragrance of Arabic biryani and lamb stew arising from it.

Huge platters of food were exchanged between families, neighbours, and friends. Sweet dishes were distributed, and people gave their fitr in the form of rice, wheat, or flour to the needy.

Zakaat was collected for poor countries, and the Muslims donated hundreds and thousands of Riyals towards charity. Requests for prayers were announced in Masjids for world peace and the Muslim Ummah, especially for those in need of relief in numerous parts of the world.

After Eid Salah, the children ate Mehalabiya and sweetmeats made with dates.

Many families visited their relative's houses. Hamza and Fariha gleefully counted the Eid money they had collected. Some of their parents' relatives and friends had also gifted them electronic games.

The day after Eid, Zuni invited Fariha, Hamza, and Khaled to her home for Eid's treat.

Farida told her children to make sure they invite Zuni and Khaled for a feast in their home the next day.

Fariha and Hamza nodded their heads and assured their mother they would extend the invitation to their friends on her behalf. After saying this, both brothers and sister set off for Zuni's house, along with Meesha.

Once they reached Zuni's house, they saw Khaled had already arrived and was chatting animatedly with Zaira.

Metallica escorted Fariha and Hamza inside. As soon as Zuni's mother saw them, she got up from the sofa and welcomed them warmly.

After wishing each other Eid Mubarak and eating their Eid-feast, the four spent the day playing.

Later in the evening, they bade each other goodbye, and Zuni and Khaled promised to visit Hamza and Fariha the next day.

CHAPTER 14- A VISIT TO THE DOHA AQUARIUM

There were only three days left of the week-long Eid Holiday. The Qatar International School planned to resume its classes from Monday onwards.

Fariha, Khaled, and Hamza had met at Zuni's home to play with the rabbits she kept in a hutch on the lawn.

However, the chief attraction for the children was Zuni's talking Macaw, Mr Tims

Zuni's lawn had a wooden treehouse and a shed that was converted into a playhouse at the bottom of their garden.

The four children were feeding almonds to Mr Tims when Metallica entered the room and informed them in her robotic voice that Zuni's mother had asked them to come down to the living room.

All four children bounded up from the floor and followed Metallica.

Zaira smiled as the children trooped in and enquired in her gentle voice, " Would you like to visit the Qatar aquarium tomorrow?"

The children felt thrilled, and they all chorused, "Yes, Shukran, we would like that very much."

Corniche was a 7km strip of waterfront that stretched in a half-moon shape around Doha Bay.

At one end of the promenade stood a sparkling white building, it was the Museum of Islamic Art. It attracted numerous visitors throughout the day.

The Museum had an incredible collection of Islamic culture, including hundreds of years old Quran scripts.

It also offered a birds-eye view over the clear waters from every conceivable angle.

At the other end of Corniche, the Qatari government had constructed the underground aquarium in 2090.
Zaira took the four children and Metallica to the entrance, where she presented their tickets to the security robot.

The moment the group entered the dark pod-like structure, they felt remarkably relaxed and distinguished the slightly damp odour associated with an aquarium.

The aquarium had over five hundred plus species with

more than nine thousand animals and plants installed over an area of more than a hundred hectares.

The aquarium boasted of having over seven million gallons of seawater.

The tropical underwater forest took the children's breath away while the main aquarium was humongous and had a transparent glass tunnel for the visitors to walk through.

Giant display glasses that enclosed oceanariums, behind which loomed sharks with intimidating sharp fangs.

Further ahead was a junction leading down a dark corridor and a sign that encouraged the visitors to swim with the sharks.

Two Giant turtles that were at least one hundred years old sat rock-still while the other younger turtles swam freely in what could only be described as oversized glass tubs.

The children could not take their eyes off the underwater coral and pressed their noses against the glass aquariums to get a better view.

Jellyfishes in purple, green and blue colours floated up and down their round tube-like transparent glass structures. The place was dark, and the only glow was the light coming from the glass displays.

At last, the group reached an auditorium that housed a gigantic speckled fish with white stripes. The immense size of the fish stunned the children, and they looked around, trying to get their bearing.

For a moment, it felt like they had entered a movie theatre, and the screen was displaying the giant fish. But only this was real, and they watched in fascination as the fish swam in and out of their vision, in its humongous allotted space.

Zaira saw the awe on the children's faces and grabbed the opportunity to tell them about Prophet Yunus (Alaihi Salaam) and the whale.

She told them how a whale swallowed Prophet Yunus (Alaihi salaam), and three layers of darkness surrounded prophet Yunus in the whale's stomach. The darkness of the whale's stomach, the darkness of the sea bottom, and the darkness of the night.

However, Almighty Allah saw the sincere repentance of Prophet Yunus and heard his invocation from the whale's stomach. Allah then commanded the whale to emerge to the surface again and put Prophet Yunus on an island.

The children listened to the story, astounded. They wondered at Prophet Yunus's state and how he must have felt in the pit of whale's stomach.

But it was Khaled who pointed out the greatest remarkable truth. He said, "Despite the Prophet being in the whale's stomach and at the bottom of the sea, Allah still heard his invocations. He took mercy upon him and responded to supplications."

Zaira felt impressed with Khaled and his insightfulness and told him, "Yes, my child. Allah will hear you even if you are buried inside the sea. He will see you even if you are inside a dark cave on a moonless night, and He can hear and see every one, even to the smallest creatures that humans cannot see or hear."

Shortly, it was time to leave the aquarium, and they all went home enamoured with the jewels of the sea like the fish, coral, and shells. Each one was a unique and beautiful creation of

Allah.

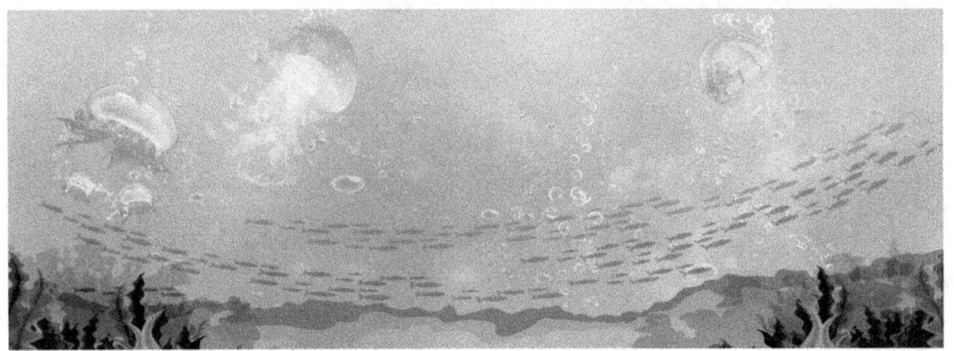

CHAPTER 15- QIS ANNOUNCEMENT

There was great excitement on Qatar International School's campus. The headmaster, Mr Roberts, had announced a poetry writing competition for the QIS students. The winner would represent the school on an international level and also win a cash prize.

There was a palpable excitement in the air, and the children excitedly discussed who would represent their class.

Hamza had signed up, and he would be representing grade three. Fariha was sure her brother would win the competition, hands down.

Hamza, from a young age, had aspired to be a writer. He maintained a diary and wrote his poems when he felt inspired. The diary was filled with poetry and short stories he wrote. His mother, Farida, treasured the moments Hamza would take her hand and make her sit next to him as he recited his poetry verses to her.

"My budding writer," his mother would lovingly say while patting his curly hair.

Haleh, a quiet girl from grade four, had added her name for the competition. Her family had moved from Kuwait two years back as Haleh's father had changed jobs and joined Qatar Airlines as a pilot.

Along with Haleh, another nine-year-old, boy named Rayyan was representing grade four.

Rayyan was sharp as a tack, but his classmates found him annoying. He loved to boast about his achievements, and he took every opportunity to make the other children feel inept about their works.

The students of class four were fed up with his arrogant behaviour but grudgingly admitted that he was the best to represent them for the poetry competition. However, everyone was silently rooting for Haleh.

From grade five, three children, Noor, Abdullah, and Shenaz represented their class.

The competition was open for the age group of eight to ten years, so from grade three to grade five, eight students were contending to get the top spot and represent their school on an international level.

During the lunch break, Hamza quickly finished his meal

and excused himself. Khaled, Fariha, and Zuni looked proudly at their friend's commitment towards the competition.

Hamza sat quietly on his desk, thinking deeply about what topic he would write. After many attempts, an idea popped into his head, and the words took shape, creating a beautiful picture. He quickly jotted down his points and picked up the threads for his theme.

The verses glided through his thoughts, similar to the electronic bricks game - Montendo, each word fitted in after the other like the digital bricks sliding down smoothly in their allotted space.

At that moment, Rayyan was walking past the grade three classroom. He peeked inside and was startled to see Hamza sitting all alone in his seat. His dark head was bent in concentration, and he was furiously writing in his digital Netbook.

Rayyan was sure that Hamza was writing his poetry piece for the competition. A tight feeling of jealousy entered his heart. He wanted to win the competition and prove that he was the best.

Rayyan looked around. There were five minutes left before the break ended. He silently sidled inside the classroom and stood in front of Hamza.

"It is no use missing your break to write your poetry. I plan to walk away with the first prize," Rayyan boasted.

Hamza looked up, surprised to see Rayyan standing before him, "What are you doing here? Go back to your classroom." Hamza frowned, irritated at Rayyan's interference in his work.

Rayyan snatched the Netbook from Hamza's hands and

said, "Let's see what you have written."

Hamza was furious. He tried to snatch his Netbook back from the bigger boy, but Rayyan had already looked through the writing with his shrewd eyes.

Rayyan shoved the digital Netbook back in Hamza's chest and said, "Have it back. Don't start moaning, and your lousy ideas are not worth my time."

Hamza scowled at Rayyan. At that moment, the bell sounded for the end of the break, and Rayyan swiftly exited the room.

CHAPTER 16 -HAMZA IN TROUBLE

Fariha, Zuni, and Khaled were walking down the corridor when they saw Rayyan running out of the third-grade classroom door. They hurried inside and found a furious Hamza clutching his digital Netbook to his chest. When Hamza told them about Rayyan's behaviour, they felt annoyed.

Fariha wanted to tell Miss Rabia, but Hamza stopped her and said it was all right.

Two days later, all eight students taking part in the poetry competition assembled in the art room to express their written work to Mr Roberts, who was sitting in one of the three chairs along with two more teachers who were part of the selection panel.

The teachers had segregated the students alphabetically according to their last names, Mr Roberts asked the students to recite the verses they had written, Rayyan Ahmed was the first, while Hamza Khoury was last.

Rayyan started his recitation; he tuned his voice to a gentle tone.

'Soft is the clouds that move with the breeze.
In the blue sky without a crease.
Soft is the morning breeze that blows through the flowers.
And soft is the dew that falls on the grass.
Soft are the petals of a flower on which descends a butterfly.

Soft is the tongue of a believer who adores his Lord's Mercy and HIS Might.

Soft is the peace that descends, following belief with words so unique.

True is the promise of Allah, for "truly in His remembrance will a heart find peace."

Soft are the words whispered in the night, calling out to the most merciful when fear has taken flight.

Soft is the mat on which rests a believer's forehead, calling in Sajdah to the Most High

Soft is the dawn when Ramadan is close by.

And soft are the eyes that read the words of the Qur'an with a sigh."

A burst of applause went around as Rayyan ended his verse, but Hamza sat in stunned silence. Those were his notes.

Rayyan had taken the lines from his Netbook and recited them word for word to the entire selection team.

Now, what was Hamza supposed to do? He could not repeat almost identical words or design during his recitation.

His mind worked furiously, and at last, he smiled. He knew what he had to do.

He opened his digital Netbook and quietly composed. Shortly, he was lost in concentration.

After almost everyone had finished, Miss Sheeba called out Hamza's name.

Hamza got up from his seat and stood in front of the students.

Rayyan was silently smirking, but Hamza spoke in a serene voice, "As you all know, my country has been at war for many years. I thought of writing this theme for people to understand what the children of war-torn countries are facing."

With his head raised high, he took a deep breath and started:

'There was no respite.
As the blazing sun shone with all its might.
The day was hot and burning white.
The young girl, Naira, felt weak with hunger.
As the cramps in her stomach stung her.
It had been many days since her family had eaten.
While her country raged with war beaten.
She was a victim of someone's misplaced sense of justice.
She was a Rohingya.
She was a Uighur.
She was a human being.
Her father had told her that it was the precious land they fought for.
And for power.
They were the people who lived in mighty towers. Little Naira did not understand what was war.
And for land, why cause destruction so much more?
Why fight for a piece of earth?
When in the end it was where they were to return.
All she wanted to have was food to eat.
All she wanted was to sleep in peace.
All she wanted was to go to school.
And without fear, go to play and dream.
She saw something outside her home.
But she knew she could not step out.
There was danger lurking at every corner.
But still, the little girl ran down the steps of her home.
It turned out to be a part of a broken plate of ceramic.
She turned to go inside, now panicked.

But coming her way was something satanic.
The feeling was strange when she felt the ground shake beneath her feet.
The weapon of destruction burst through her house.
But Miraculously, she was saved.
But unfortunately, it was her home that was caved.
She turned in shock to see her humble, broken-down home.
It had shattered, and now it was nothing more.
But a pile of debris.
Poor Naira couldn't breathe for an eternity.
The shock wasn't the sight of the pile of stones and bricks.
The fragments of her shattered home.
They were too many in her country.
Her country was Yemen. Syria, or maybe Palestine.
It was the country that was at war.
It was an extremely common sight to behold.
Houses and lives shattered when bombarded with tales untold.
But the shock was greater than a destroyed home.
Her Baba, Ammi, and her brother and sister were now all under the heap of rubble.
She clawed at the rocks helplessly.
But her tiny hands were useless against the massive mountain that now stood passively.
Little Naira was shocked and then felt confusion.
Alas, she felt lost amongst the chaos.
From whom she could have got answers, lost to her call.
Her father was so strong and big.
And her mother, so kind and sweet.
Never would her brother swing her in his arms again.
Nor would her sister teasingly pull the ribbon from her hair.
Gone were the people she called family.
This little girl called Naira is from a war-torn country called Iraq, Syria, Yemen, or Afghanistan.
For all the war-torn countries seem alike.
With homes crushed into rubble and families destroyed.
Her father had said once that the men fought and planned.

But for little Naira, she would give away all the land.
If only she could get her family back.
She cried and refused to move from the place she once called home.
Calling with futility to her Abbu and Ammi.
Oh, how she mourned.
Till another bolt of light flashed through the air.
Causing a whizzing sound.
As it crashed.
This time, little Naira couldn't get away.
As beautiful angels took her away.
She saw the open sky with land so green.
The palace glimmered in the distant.
With her Baba and Ammi dressed in clothes resplendent.
Her beloved brother and sister, laughing and shining like stars in the distant sky.
Little Naira understood at last as she flew with joy.
As the doors of heaven opened in the yonder.
That what she had left behind was a load too heavy for others to bear.
As for her.....
Peace, at last, was very near.

As Hamza ended his poetry, not a single dry eye was left in the room. Mr Roberts was quietly wiping his hands over his eyes while Miss Sheeba had tears running down her face.

Rayyan sat silently, feeling ashamed and unable to meet Hamza's eyes.

Once Hamza finished, Mr Roberts spoke in his deep voice and mentioned that the winners would be announced next Monday during assembly in front of the entire school.

The group of students streamed out and went back to their respective classes.

A week later, the results were announced in the assembly hall. It was a tie between Hamza and Rayyan.

The committee members had decided to have another round of submissions between the two boys.

Hamza felt disappointed because he knew both the poems were his. He then put up his hands and prayed to Allah to sort the matter, "Ya Allah! I put my trust in you and keep my patience, waiting for your help."

After the lunch break, Hamza was asked to go to Mr Roberts' room. He knocked on the door and heard the deep voice of the headmaster asking him to come in.

Hamza entered with his heart beating in trepidation. He had not yet prepared his new poetry, and he hoped he was not expected to submit his work immediately.

Mr Roberts received the boy with a grave face. Hamza felt his heart sinking to his feet.

Mr Roberts then asked him to sit and cleared his throat as he was about to speak, "Hamza, Rayyan visited me after the assembly. The boy was very distressed, and he confessed to copying your work from your Netbook. I want to ask why did you not speak up when you heard Rayyan recite your written work?"

Hamza turned red with embarrassment and said shame-facedly, "I felt scared to say anything. I thought you wouldn't believe me."

Seeing the young boy's distress, Mr Roberts spoke gently, " My son. In life, you will come across many Rayyans who will take credit for your hard work, and if you don't learn to stand up for your rights, you would be encouraging the oppressor to continue his bullying. Remember, Hamza, the one who keeps quiet is worse than the oppressor."

Hamza nodded his head, and the headmaster's direct words made him see his situation plainly for what it was.

Mr Roberts' eyes now twinkled merrily behind his glasses, and he said in a cheerful voice at once, putting Hamza at ease, "Looks like you are the clear winner as both poetries are your work. I will be announcing this in the assembly tomorrow. I wish you all the best."

After school was over, Hamza, Fariha, Zuni and Khaled went in Zuni's Aerocar zooming over the rooftops.

Hamza told his friends about his conversation with the headmaster.

"Good for you, Hamza," Fariha squealed in delight.

Khaled thumped his friends and grinned.

Zuni laughed and said, "Oohhh, we are sitting with a winner."

Hamza was delighted with their reaction, and he grinned widely, "Now, wish me the best for the international competition, and pray that I do not encounter another Rayyan."

All four friends uproariously laughed while Metallica veered the Aerocar expertly over the Corniche.

CHAPTER 17-A VISIT TO THE ANIMAL PARK

Hamza, Zuni, Khaled and Fariha were excited about the upcoming trip with their families to the animal and bird park in Al Khuraib.

Even though it was a long drive from their home, their mothers had planned the trip so the children could experience the fantastic park with their many animals replete with futuristic technology.

The animal park stretched across one hundred and fifty hectares of land.

Zaira had hired a future-Gen Van which ran on hydro jet fuel and ensured a smooth and comfortable ride. It was spacious enough to fit all three families together.

All three mothers; Zaira, Farida, and Araba would be in charge of the group. Metallica would also be a part of the outing as she could help with the picnic.

After Fajr, just as the sun rose over the horizon, the van arrived at Zuni's home.

Zuni and Khaled were neighbours, so Khaled's mother, Araba, his eleven-year-old sister, Ruqaiya and his two-year-old twin siblings, Sara and Abrar, with their nanny, Teresa, waited with Zuni and Zaira at their gate.

Zuni's elder brothers wouldn't be accompanying the group to Qur'an Garden because they had planned to spend the day with their father at a camel farm.

Araba and Zaira's families, their maids, and Metallica got inside the van and took their seats amongst asymmetrical seats near the glass windows.

A giant monitor displayed safety information and later switched onto talking about the outside temperature.

Once everyone had been accounted for, the van left their street to pick up Fariha, Hamza, and their mother, Farida.

Farida stood at their apartment gate with Hamza and Fariha. They all waited excitedly for the others to pick them up.

Metallica got down from the van to help them with their picnic things.

The Future-Zen vehicle started noiselessly and zoomed down the road towards the Animal and bird park.

CHAPTER 18- INSIDE THE ANIMAL PARK

The wrought-iron gates of Doha Zoological gardens swung automatically when the van approached the entrance.

The gates looked magnificent with massive white pillars on both sides of the entrance. At first glance, the children saw dense trees before them but once the canopy of trees ended, the sheer size of the wildlife park stunned the children.

A vast ground lay before them shaded with giant oak and Cedar trees. Their branches forked and spread out entwining with other trees forming a tunnel. Over the tunnel names of sections were displayed.

The Amazon section displayed information on pythons and giant spiders. Another section had the Cold-North written on it and one could see Penguins and Polar Bears. Each section covered a part of the world with its unique species.

Zaira explained to the group that the park had a layout with enclosed sections housing wild animals like the golden sub-nosed monkeys from China, Giant Pandas, Meerkat, False Gharial, lama, a Sumatran Orangutan, Indian Muntjac, Red Ruffed Lemur and many more.

Some of the prominent animals like the elephant and tiger had gone extinct some fifty years back, so there were virtual reality images of them roaming freely in the park along with T-Rex,

Triceratops, Velociraptor and Stegosaurus.

The children could hear robotic narrators on speakers as they repeated feeding times and information about the animals.

Zuni gasped in awe and pointed out as a massive velociraptor roared passed them.

Khaled noticed the picnic area had built-in stone grills with community marble tables and seats. A Bengal tiger's virtual image with its amazing black stripes and orange fur roamed amongst the grounds. It looked at Khaled and roared deafeningly, making the boy hurry after his family.

Fariha and Zuni saw kids shrieking in joy while sliding down a long rainbow slide. The playgrounds came equipped with the latest swings, zip-lines, and seesaw, but the kids knew they had to move ahead.

As soon as they entered the main pathway, the security greeted the group with the customary Islamic greeting of 'Assalaam alaikum.' The mothers guided the children towards the lawn area, and a robot with an electronic golf cart approached the group.

Hamza hopped inside and helped Nanny Teresa with Sara and Abrar. The others got in one by one, and the golf cart began the wildlife park rounds.

The first stop was meeting Mimi the Orangutan. Fariha, Hamza, Khaled and Zuni took turns in clicking pictures with the friendly Mimi. When Sara and Abrar sat with Mimi, the Orangutan pulled Abrar's ears and made him cry.

Nanny Teresa scolded Mimi who put her paws over her eyes while her keeper grinned at the mischievous chimp.

They decided to walk to the next exhibit and thanked the robot with the golf cart for his service.

Tall white heads loomed from an enclosure while Fariha squealed in delight, looking at the llama. One bounded within the enclosure with its long limbs, and another came near the group and put its head out.

Another group of children had come with their parents. One boy stood with his tuft of wild-looking hair close to the llama's enclosure. The llama thinking the boy's hair resembled the dry hay, its favourite food, and it took a mouthful of the hair in its mouth. The boy wailed when he felt his hair was stuck in the llama's mouth.

Hamza heard the father say, "Atiq, next time, listen to your mother when she says you need to comb your hair."

Hamza hastily got away from the llama's enclosure and ran a protective hand over his headful of thick hair.

In the middle of the fun moments, the children went to pet a giraffe who tried to lick Fariha with its long sticky tongue. Fariha laughed and patted its neck.

They also saw the adorable Panda, and it was feeding time for them. The children went to the caretaker, who gave them bamboo shoots to feed the fluffy animals.

The next stop was the Red Ruffed Lemur, and the proboscis nosed monkey.

However, Araba wanted to take a break with the two toddlers as both were cranky and wanted to eat their meal. Ruqaiya stayed behind with her mother and Nanny Teresa to help Araba.

Zaira and Farida proceeded with the group in the direction of the red-ruffed lemur. Hamza read the information board and exclaimed the lemur with the fiery red fur had come to meet them all the way from Madagascar.

After meeting the lemur, the group broke for lunch. Zaira removed her phone from her purse and mentioned Araba's name in the speaker. Araba's virtual image appeared, and Zaira spoke to her about meeting in the community garden.

Fariha and Zuni walked together, while Khaled and Hamza raced each other and moved ahead of the group.

Farida and Zaira brought up the rear walking sedately while they recounted the incredible modifications they had seen in the park since their last visit five years back.

For lunch, the group sat at the community table while Teresa and Metallica laid out the spread. There were Machboos with chicken and lamb Thareed, as well as kebabs and Fatayer. It all ended with the sweet Luqaimat.

Teresa also enjoyed the meal while Metallica looked longingly at the feast. Poor Metallica, the robot was not programmed to digest the food that humans ate.

Zaira said, "Thank Allah, even though almost everything's changed in Qatar, but the traditional food tastes just as delicious as before."

The others agreed heartily with Zaira as they packed the leftover food and helped Metallica and Teresa clean the mess.

CHAPTER 19- SARA AND ABRAR

After clearing the meal, the group wanted to explore and have more fun at the park.

They got up from the table, and at that point, Araba exclaimed in shock, "Where are Sara and Abrar?"

In a moment, there was confusion as everybody started searching for the twins. Araba was in tears, and the others were tensed when they could not find the twins.

The robot security immediately fanned out their sensors to search for the toddlers.

The group then heard an announcement instructing them to move towards the virtual elephant section.

The robot security had found Sara and Abrar trying to mount a patiently-waiting elephant image.

Araba hugged her two naughty but adorable kids and thanked Allah for protecting them.

After the fuss caused by Sara and Abrar was resolved the group moved towards the Cold-North section.
Fariha and Zuni skipped ahead in the Humboldt Penguins' direction, and they entered the chilled enclosed room.

The penguins were in a water tank shaped like the cold region where they came from. They were funny to watch, and Sara clapped her hands, looking at the comical creatures.

The flightless birds flapped their wings and dived deep into their clear water tank.

After spending nearly half-hour in the room, the children were reluctant to leave the Penguin show, but Farida urged them to check the Zebra section.

As the sun went low on the horizon, the group of elders and children offered their `Asr Salah in the wildlife park.

The evening sun was preparing to go into hiding, and it was time to go back home.

Before getting on the Van, the mothers fussed over the children as they counted and confirmed their presence twice.

After Metallica handed the twins to Nanny Teresa and Araba, Sara and Abrar settled in their seats close to their nanny and mother.

Hamza, Fariha, Khaled and Zuni then went in next.

One by one, the group got in the Van. Metallica got in last and took her seat.

The Van's automatic sensor doors shut behind her. After one last look at the lovely park area from their seats, the van started and slowly wound its way out of the wrought-iron gates.

The mothers heaved a sigh and thanked Allah for a beautiful day. The children, drained out after the excitement, sat peacefully and relived the wonderful moments amongst themselves.

As the Van dropped each family at their homes, they

said a tired goodbye to others.

Once Fariha got home, she excitedly told her father about the experience. Meesha came and rubbed against Fariha's legs, beseechingly meowing for being left behind by her young mistress.

Fariha picked up Meesha, who seemed to be in a huff, and said, "Next time, Meesha. I promise to take you with me to the wildlife park, but I do hope the robots don't mistake you for one of the animals in their enclosures."

CHAPTER 20- SANDSTORM

Warnings rang out from the drones that circled Doha about an approaching sandstorm. Transparent glass domes appeared all over the city as the Qatari people pressed the button on their remote control that activated glass shields to cover their homes from the rage of the storm.

People living in apartments activated window shields and sat back waiting for the storm to hit their city. A low whistling sound could be heard, and then the sound became louder as the wind picked up speed.

Fariha, Khaled, Zuni and Hamza watched dark heavy clouds approaching their city from afar. The next moment they realized it was the sand whirling in the wind that had covered the entire horizon.

The sand swirled outside the dome as it sped over the transparent glass. The children were in Zuni's home when the drones flew out with their warnings.

Zuni's mother ordered Alexa to call Hamza's mother, and through her virtual image, she informed her the children were safe in their home.

Khaled also decided to stay back, and Alexa connected him with his family. He waved to Sara and Abrar, who excitedly tried to catch his virtual image but came up empty-handed.

Metallica whirled out with a tray filled with Baklava and Sherbet. Khaled immediately took the tray from the robot and thanked her.

Zuni's mother came out to sit with the children and watch the sky turn to gold as grains of sand swirled over their heads.

Zuni asked her mother if the storm could die out by evening. Zaira looked into her daughter's dark, intense, eyes and replied, "Insha Allah, my child."

Fariha sucked in her breath as the storm's fury uprooted a date palm tree that flew over the dome.

Hamza curiously asked Zuni's mother, "Was there ever a day like this when you were stuck in your home and could not go out?"

Zaira smiled and said her grandmother had told her stories about people being quarantined in their homes. She mentioned her grandmother had heard the stories from her mother about the COVID-19 story.

"At one time, my great grandmother and her family faced months in confinement, and they couldn't leave their homes."
The children exclaimed together, "When was that?"

Zuni pleaded with her mother to tell them about what had happened.

Zaira reminisced about her childhood moments spent in the company of her grandmother and the stories and wisdom she had shared with her.

Zaira started, "It was the year 2019, and a virus had spread in all parts of the world. No one could step out of their homes for months until the virus was brought under control. The entire city of Doha was shut, not a shop was open, and not even the Mosques.

Men and women prayed their Salah at home. Even Ramadan was spent indoors, and no food was exchanged for the fear of spreading the virus.

Tarawih was again observed at home, and no one stepped out. The roads were deserted, and the time came to a standstill.

Millions of people had perished all over the world and many more faced after-effects of the disease as it had affected their lungs and breathing system.

But Alhamdulillah, Allah had mercy on the world and slowly, the people limped back to normal times, and the virus went away."

On hearing the story, the children realised how fortunate they were that the virus was no longer in the world.

Zuni's mother soothingly said, "Even though the world was in a perilous condition Muslims kept Sabr and Shukr because is not the virus nothing more than Qadr Allah."

After Maghreb Salah the storm died down, and Hamad came to pick up Fariha and Hamza in his car to take them home.

CHAPTER 21-THE FOOTBALL SEASON

All over the world, the FIFA World Cup fever had taken the people by storm. Khaled rooted for his favourite football world cup player, Hussain Al Zoher.

In school, football matches were announced, and Khaled was the forward player.

In another three weeks, the world cup would be played in their city, and the streets would be empty. The stadium had taken years to be ready for this event. Hotels were booked in advance, and the city of Doha had taken a festive look.

Buntings with the FIFA logo hung in the malls and stores.

Khaled and his team had played against another rival school in the inter-school football tournament, and Khaled's team walked away with the trophy.

Now, if only the Qatar team would win the World Cup, Khaled's happiness would be complete.

Khaled's father and Khaled had attended all the matches for all the twenty-seven days.

Khaled would boast about the matches to Fariha, Zuni and Hamza and his other classmates.

Zuni observed that Khaled would speak out in great detail

about the players and the VIP stand that his father had booked for the duration of the FIFA cup.

Zuni also observed how Hamza looked crestfallen because his father could not afford the tickets to the stadium let alone the VIP stand.

Hamza and his family watched the live broadcast on their television.

Back in school Khaled would boast and brag and Hamza grew quieter in his friend's presence.

One day Zuni saw how Khaled exaggerated about the VIP stand and the amazing food they were served complimentary. Then Khaled removed a book and in it was the autograph of the best-loved Qatar player Hussain Al Zoher.

Hamza was pleased for his friend and congratulated Khaled on getting the autograph.

However, Khaled said tactlessly, "Too bad Hamza you cannot enjoy the match like the others at the stadium."

CHAPTER 23-KHALED LEARNS A LESSON IN HUMILITY

One or two other children snickered and Hamza abruptly got up and went away.

Zuni was furious with Khaled. She too got up and went after Hamza and Fariha who had walked out the moment her brother had left the room.

Khaled was left behind in the room holding the book with Hussain Al Zoher's signature. A few boys laughed and said maybe Hamza was jealous of Khaled.

Khaled turned furiously to face the sneering boys and told them to shut up.

Khaled ran after his friends and caught up with Zuni who was standing a little distance away watching Fariha talk to her brother.

When Khaled stood next to her Zuni turned to face him furiously, "Khaled, you have been boasting non-stop about your VIP seats without taking Hamza's feelings in contemplation, now see how you hurt his self-respect by insulting him about his financial situation in front of the other boys." How do you think he must feel?" Zuni lashed out at Khaled.

Khaled at once realized his mistake and felt ashamed at his behaviour.

He advanced ahead and stood in front of Hamza, "I am sorry brother, please forgive me, I guess I had lost my head in the frenzy of the football season."

Hamza at once forgave Khaled for his insensitive remarks and the two boys shook hands.

Zuni and Fariha heaved a sigh of relief for they did not want the boys to be at loggerheads over a sports match.

CHAPTER 24- FIFA THE FINAL MATCH

The last day of the match approached, it was the final, Qatar had sailed through the season and was up against the France team.

Hamza had decided to watch the match with Ameer on the television because his father was working on an important assignment.

It was a given that he would be working late and watch the match on the giant office screen in the conference room with his other two colleagues who would be working that day.

Most of the others had taken the day off to see the match.

Unfortunately for Hamza, Ameer too could not join his brother, so it was only Hamza alone.

Fariha would be there but Hamza knew it was only to please him.

His mother was not interested in the football match or any sports matches.

The doorbell rang and Hamza went to open the lock.

He was astounded to find Khaled standing outside, grinning wide and waving in his hands what looked like airline tickets.

Get ready you doofus, you are going for the final match with me." Khaled gave a friendly punch on Hamza's shoulder.

Hamza could hardly contain his excitement and he went to tell his mother about Khaled's invitation to the stadium.

Khaled had got passes for Fariha and Hamza both and their mother was pleased to see her children go and enjoy themselves at the stadium.

Khaled's father had booked the VIP gallery for Khaled and his friends. His family would all be going in Khaled's father Aerocar.

Metallica would drive Zuni's Aerocar, with Zuni, Hamza, Khaled, and Fariha as its passengers.

The stadium was packed and the crowd went crazy roaring for Qatar team to win the match.

The match was exciting to watch as Qatar played against France and scored two goals.

The crowd watched with bated breath as the players gathered on the field for the final playoff. Only two minutes remained of the match and the winning team would be announced the winner.

And Hussain Al Zoher scored the winning goal taking Qatar to victory in the final match and winning the world cup.

The crowd roared and Hamza could hardly contain his excitement.

Finally, his dream had come true and Qatar had won the world cup and Hamza felt elated that he was there to watch this historic match live in the stadium.

After a wonderful day Hamza, Khaled, Fariha and Zuni got into the aero-car with Metallica and zoomed away into the horizon talking excitedly about one of the most significant days in their lives.

THE END

www.ingramcontent.com/pod-product-compliance
Lightning Source LLC
Chambersburg PA
CBHW051450150726
48000CB00005B/2332